Dings n Dongs

Behind the Doors, Volume 1

Pratham Prateek Mohanty

Published by Writistic Studios, 2024.

This is a work of fiction. Similarities to real people, places, or events are entirely coincidental.

DINGS N DONGS

First edition. March 3, 2024.

ISBN: 979-8224920235

Written by Pratham Prateek Mohanty.

Content

Preface:

Dear Reader,

Welcome to the world of "Dings n Dongs." As you embark on this journey, prepare to step into the shadows of a world where mystery reigns supreme and every corner holds a secret waiting to be uncovered. Within these pages, you will encounter the story of Maya, a young woman whose curiosity leads her down a path fraught with danger and discovery.

As the author of this tale, it is my privilege to guide you through the twists and turns of Maya's journey as she unravels the enigma behind the abandoned house at the end of her street. But be warned: the secrets hidden within its walls are not easily revealed, and danger lurks around every corner. Will Maya uncover the truth, or will she become ensnared in the web of mystery that surrounds her?

Join me as we delve into the heart of the unknown, where the answers lie behind the dings and dongs.

Sincerely,

Pratham Prateek Mohanty

Founder & CEO

Writistic Studios

Content Rating and Advisory

This ebook, "Dings n Dongs," has been rated T (Teen) by the Writistic Content Certification Board (WCCB). It contains content suitable for readers aged 12 and above. While the themes and content may be suitable for teen readers, parental guidance is advised for readers under the age of 12 due to mild violence, suspenseful situations, and themes of mystery and psychological intrigue. Reader discretion is advised.

Regards
Ishita Choudhuri
Content Validator
WCCB, Writistic Studios

Introduction:

In the quiet suburban neighborhood of Willow Creek, where the streets are lined with neatly trimmed lawns and the houses exude an air of tranquility, lies a secret shrouded in mystery. Behind the facade of normalcy, hidden away at the end of a deserted street, stands an abandoned house - a relic of a forgotten past, its windows boarded up and its doors locked tight. But within its walls lies a tale waiting to be told, a story of secrets, intrigue, and the echoes of a bygone era.

Chapter 1: The Beginning of the Journey

The gentle glow of the moon cast an ethereal light over the sleepy suburban neighborhood of Willow Creek. Shadows danced across the neatly manicured lawns, and the occasional rustle of leaves echoed through the night. In one of the houses on Birch Street, Maya lay nestled beneath her cozy blankets, the soft hum of the city lulling her into a state of relaxation.

But as the clock struck midnight, Maya's peaceful slumber was abruptly shattered by a faint, persistent sound. It was a sound she couldn't quite place at first—a distant chime, like the tinkling of bells carried on the wind. Groggy and disoriented,

Maya blinked away the remnants of sleep and sat up in bed, straining her ears to identify the source of the mysterious sound.

At first, Maya dismissed it as a figment of her imagination—a trick of the mind brought on by the late hour. But as the chime continued to echo through the stillness of the night, growing louder and more insistent with each passing moment, Maya's curiosity got the better of her.

Throwing back the covers, Maya swung her legs over the edge of the bed and planted her feet on the cool wooden floor. She paused for a moment, listening intently as the chime reverberated through the house once more. With a determined frown, Maya pushed herself to her feet and padded across the room, her footsteps muffled by the plush carpet beneath her.

As she reached the doorway, Maya hesitated, her hand hovering over the light switch. Part of her wanted to flick on the lights, banishing the darkness and the eerie chime that seemed to fill the air. But another part of her—the part that thrived on mystery and adventure—urged her to embrace the unknown, to venture into the darkness and uncover the truth.

With a silent resolve, Maya made her decision. Ignoring the trembling in her fingers, she reached out and flipped the light switch, flooding the room with a warm, comforting glow. The sudden burst of light banished the shadows that had lurked in the corners, dispelling the sense of unease that had settled over Maya like a heavy shroud.

Taking a deep breath to steady her nerves, Maya stepped out into the hallway, her footsteps echoing softly on the polished floorboards. The chime grew louder as she moved closer to the source, guiding her like a beacon through the labyrinth of her house. It seemed to be coming from downstairs—the front door, perhaps, or the foyer.

With each step, Maya's heart pounded in her chest, a mixture of excitement and apprehension coursing through her veins. She couldn't shake the feeling that something important was about to happen—that her life was about to change in ways she couldn't yet comprehend.

As Maya descended the staircase, the chime grew louder still, its melody weaving through the air like a siren's call. With each passing moment, Maya felt herself drawn inexorably toward the source, her curiosity overriding any sense of caution or doubt.

Finally, she reached the ground floor and stood before the front door, her hand trembling slightly as she reached out to grasp the handle. For a moment, she hesitated, her mind racing with a thousand questions and possibilities. But then, with a firm resolve, she twisted the handle and swung the door open, revealing the moonlit world beyond.

And there, standing on the threshold of her home, Maya was greeted by a sight that took her breath away—a sight that would set into motion a chain of events that would change her life forever.

For standing before her, bathed in the soft glow of the moon, was a figure unlike any Maya had ever seen before—a figure cloaked in shadow, its features obscured by darkness. And as Maya gazed into its inscrutable eyes, she felt a shiver run down her spine, a sense of foreboding creeping over her like a chill wind on a winter's night.

But despite the fear that gripped her heart, Maya knew that she could not turn away—not now, not when she stood on the brink of discovery. With a steady hand and a resolute gaze, she stepped forward into the night, ready to confront whatever lay beyond the threshold of her home.

For Maya had always been drawn to the unknown—to the mysteries that lurked in the shadows, waiting to be uncovered. And now, as she stood on the threshold of a new adventure, she knew that she was about to embark on the journey of a lifetime—a journey that would take her beyond the boundaries of her imagination, into a world where anything was possible.

And so, with a silent prayer on her lips and a sense of determination in her heart, Maya took her first steps into the darkness, ready to face whatever lay ahead. For she knew that no matter what trials awaited her, she would face them with courage and conviction, guided by the light of her own indomitable spirit.

And as the door swung shut behind her, sealing her fate and plunging her into the depths of the unknown, Maya knew that her adventure had only just begun.

Chapter 2: Into the Unknown

The moon hung like a silver orb in the midnight sky, casting its ethereal glow over the quiet streets of Willow Creek. Maya stood at the threshold of the abandoned house, her pulse racing in her ears as she gazed up at the looming structure before her. The once-grand mansion now stood as a ghostly relic, its windows boarded up and its facade weathered by time.

With each step she took, the weight of the night pressed down upon her, a palpable sense of foreboding settling over the neighborhood. Yet, despite the overwhelming silence that surrounded her, Maya's curiosity burned bright within her chest, driving her forward into the unknown.

Pushing open the rusted gate, Maya stepped onto the cracked pavement that led to the front door. The air was thick with the scent of decay, and the only sound was the soft whisper of the wind as it rustled through the overgrown foliage.

As she approached the door, Maya's heart pounded in her chest, the sound echoing in her ears like a drumbeat of anticipation. With trembling fingers, she reached out and grasped the tarnished handle, her breath catching in her throat as she pushed the door open.

The interior of the abandoned house was cloaked in darkness, the only light coming from the faint glow of the moon filtering in through the dust-covered windows. Shadows danced across the walls, casting strange shapes that seemed to shift and writhe in the dim light.

Taking a hesitant step forward, Maya ventured into the foyer, her eyes scanning the dilapidated surroundings. Cobwebs hung from the ceiling like tattered curtains, and the floorboards creaked beneath her weight, protesting the intrusion of her footsteps.

With each room she explored, Maya felt the weight of the house's history pressing down upon her. She imagined the lives that had once inhabited these walls, the laughter and tears that had echoed through these halls, now lost to the passage of time.

As she made her way through the abandoned rooms, Maya's senses were heightened, every creak of the floorboards, every rustle of the curtains sending shivers down her spine. Yet, she pressed on, driven by an insatiable curiosity to uncover the secrets that lay hidden within the house's walls.

Finally, after what felt like an eternity of searching, Maya came upon a door at the end of a long hallway. It stood slightly ajar, a sliver of light spilling out from the crack. With a trembling hand, she pushed it open, revealing a room bathed in an otherworldly glow.

Inside, Maya found herself standing in what appeared to be a study, the air thick with the scent of old books and parchment. A desk sat against one wall, covered in a layer of dust and cobwebs, upon which sat an ancient-looking journal.

With trembling fingers, Maya reached out and picked up the journal, her heart pounding in her chest as she flipped open the weathered cover. The pages were yellowed with age, the ink faded and smudged, but the words were clear and legible.

As she began to read, Maya felt a chill run down her spine. The journal contained the secrets of the abandoned house, detailing its dark history and the tragic events that had unfolded within its walls. Each word sent a shiver of fear down her spine, yet Maya couldn't tear her eyes away from the pages, captivated by the tale of horror and despair that unfolded before her.

But before Maya could delve deeper into the journal's secrets, a sudden noise shattered the silence, causing her to jump in alarm. She glanced up, her heart pounding in her chest, and froze as she saw a shadowy figure looming in the doorway.

Chapter 3: Echoes of the Past

Maya's heart hammered against her ribcage as she faced the imposing figure in the doorway. The dim light cast eerie shadows across his features, accentuating the intensity in his eyes.

"Susej?" Maya's voice trembled as she spoke, uncertainty lacing her words.

The man inclined his head slightly in acknowledgment, his gaze never wavering from Maya's face. "Yes, that is my name," he confirmed, his voice deep and resonant, sending shivers down Maya's spine.

Maya's mind raced, grappling with a whirlwind of questions. Who was this man, and why was he here? What connection did he have to the abandoned house and the mysterious doorbell?

Before Maya could gather her thoughts, Susej took a step forward, closing the distance between them. His presence seemed to fill the room, commanding attention and instilling a sense of unease in Maya.

"What brings you to this place, Maya?" Susej's voice was calm, but there was an underlying intensity that sent a chill down Maya's spine.

Maya swallowed hard, her mouth suddenly dry. "I... I heard the doorbell," she admitted, her voice barely above a whisper. "I followed the sound here, hoping to uncover its source."

Susej regarded her with a penetrating gaze, his expression unreadable. "Ah, the doorbell," he mused, as if lost in thought. "It has a way of drawing people in, doesn't it? But not everyone who seeks its source is prepared for what they may find."

Maya's heart raced at his words, a knot of fear tightening in her chest. What did he mean? What secrets lay hidden within the abandoned house?

"What do you mean?" Maya asked, her voice trembling slightly.

Susej's lips curved into a faint smile, but there was no warmth in it. "The doorbell is more than just a sound, Maya," he explained cryptically. "It is a doorway to a realm beyond our own, where reality bends and twists in ways you cannot imagine."

Maya's head spun with confusion, her mind struggling to comprehend Susej's cryptic words. A realm beyond their own? It seemed impossible, absurd even. And yet, there was something in Susej's demeanor that told her he was not speaking in riddles.

Before Maya could press him for answers, Susej turned and began to walk away, his form melting into the shadows like a ghost. "Wait!" Maya called out, her voice echoing through the empty room. But there was no response, only the faint echo of her own words lingering in the air.

Alone once more, Maya was left with more questions than answers. Who was Susej, and what did he know about the doorbell? And most importantly, what secrets lay hidden within the abandoned house, waiting to be uncovered?

With a heavy heart and a mind full of uncertainty, Maya knew that her journey was far from over. And as she stood in the darkness, the faint echo of the doorbell still ringing in her ears, Maya knew that she was about to embark on an adventure unlike any she had ever known.

And so, with determination burning in her heart, Maya steeled herself for the challenges that lay ahead, ready to uncover the truth behind the mysteries of the abandoned house and the enigmatic figure known as Susej.

Chapter 4: Veil of Shadows

Maya stood alone in the dimly lit room, the echoes of her own words reverberating through the empty space. The encounter with Susej had left her shaken, her mind swirling with questions and uncertainty. But despite her apprehension, a stubborn curiosity gnawed at her, driving her deeper into the heart of the mystery.

Taking a deep breath to steady her nerves, Maya turned her attention back to the ancient journal lying open on the dusty desk. With trembling hands, she reached out and began to leaf through its pages once more, her eyes scanning the faded text in search of answers.

As she read, Maya felt a chill run down her spine. The journal spoke of a time long ago, when the abandoned house had been a place of joy and laughter, filled with the sounds of children's laughter and the warmth of family gatherings. But beneath the surface, darkness lurked, waiting to be unleashed.

The entries grew increasingly ominous as Maya delved deeper into the journal's pages. Tales of strange occurrences and unexplained phenomena filled the pages, painting a picture of a house haunted by its own past. Maya's pulse quickened as she read of mysterious disappearances and whispered rumors of a malevolent presence that lurked within the shadows.

But amid the darkness, there were glimmers of hope. The journal spoke of a brave soul who had dared to confront the evil that dwelled within the abandoned house, risking everything in search of redemption. His name was James, a name that sent a shiver down Maya's spine.

Could James hold the key to unraveling the mystery of the abandoned house? And if so, what had become of him? Maya's mind raced with possibilities as she continued to scour the journal for clues.

Suddenly, a faint sound broke the silence, causing Maya to jump in alarm. It was the unmistakable sound of a doorbell ringing, echoing through the empty halls of the abandoned house.

Heart pounding, Maya leaped to her feet and dashed towards the source of the sound. With each step, the ringing grew louder, filling the air with an eerie sense of foreboding. Finally, she reached the front door and threw it open, expecting to find Susej waiting on the other side.

But to her surprise, the doorway was empty, the street outside bathed in moonlight. Confusion washed over Maya as she stepped outside, the chill of the night air sending shivers down her spine.

And then, in the distance, she saw him - a figure standing in the shadows, watching her with dark, piercing eyes. It was Susej, his form obscured by the darkness, a silent sentinel in the night.

"Who are you?" Maya called out, her voice trembling with fear and uncertainty.

But Susej said nothing, his gaze unwavering as he disappeared into the night, leaving Maya alone once more with nothing but her questions and the echoes of the past.

As she stood in the moonlit street, Maya knew that her journey was far from over. The mysteries of the abandoned house still lay waiting to be unraveled, and she was determined to uncover the truth, no matter what dangers lay in her path.

And with a newfound sense of determination, Maya set off into the night, the echoes of the doorbell ringing in her ears, guiding her towards a destiny she could scarcely imagine.

Chapter 5: Whispers of the Ancients

The dim light filtering through the cracked windows cast long shadows across the dusty floor of the abandoned house. Maya stood alone in the silence, the weight of Susej's cryptic words lingering in the air like a heavy fog. With each passing moment, the sense of unease that gripped her tightened its hold, urging her to uncover the truth hidden within the walls of the derelict building.

Taking a deep breath to steady her nerves, Maya began to explore the abandoned house once more. Every creak of the floorboards beneath her feet echoed through the empty rooms, each shadow seeming to dance in the flickering light. She moved with cautious determination, her senses heightened as she searched for any clues that might shed light on the mysteries surrounding the house.

As Maya ventured deeper into the heart of the abandoned building, she came across a series of old photographs scattered across a dusty table. With trembling hands, she picked up the faded images, studying them with a mixture of curiosity and trepidation. The photographs depicted scenes from another time - smiling faces frozen in moments of joy, families gathered together in front of the grand fireplace, and children playing in the overgrown garden.

But as Maya studied the photographs more closely, she noticed something unsettling lurking beneath the surface. In each image, there was a subtle sense of unease, a shadow that seemed to hover at the edges of the frame. Faces twisted in fear, eyes haunted by unseen horrors - it was as if the house itself held a dark secret that it was desperate to conceal.

With a sinking feeling in the pit of her stomach, Maya realized that she was not alone in the abandoned house. The echoes of the past reverberated through the empty halls, whispering tales of tragedy and loss. But amid the darkness, there was also a glimmer of hope - a flicker of light that beckoned Maya forward, urging her to continue her quest for the truth.

Determined to uncover the secrets hidden within the abandoned house, Maya pressed on, her footsteps echoing through the empty rooms. With each passing moment, the sense of foreboding that hung in the air grew stronger, but Maya refused to be deterred. She knew that she was on the brink of a discovery that would change everything - and she was determined to see it through to the end.

As Maya moved deeper into the heart of the abandoned house, she couldn't shake the feeling that she was being watched. Shadows danced on the walls, and strange whispers seemed to echo through the empty halls. But despite the growing sense of unease, Maya pressed on, her curiosity driving her forward.

Finally, after what felt like hours of searching, Maya stumbled upon a door hidden at the end of a long, dark hallway. It stood slightly ajar, a sliver of light spilling out from the crack. With a trembling hand, Maya pushed it open, revealing a room bathed in an ethereal glow.

Inside, she found herself standing in what appeared to be a library, its shelves lined with row upon row of dusty books. But as Maya approached, she realized that these were no ordinary books - they were journals, each one filled with handwritten notes and faded memories.

With a sense of trepidation, Maya reached out and picked up one of the journals, flipping through its yellowed pages. As she read, her heart sank with each word, for the journal contained the heartbreaking tale of the family who had once called this house their home. It spoke of love and loss, of joy and sorrow - and of a darkness that had consumed them all.

As Maya read on, she felt a chill run down her spine, for she knew that the answers she sought lay within these pages. But as she delved deeper into the mysteries of the abandoned house, she couldn't shake the feeling that she was treading on dangerous ground. The echoes of the past whispered tales of tragedy and despair, and Maya knew that she was about to uncover secrets that had long been buried.

But despite the growing sense of unease, Maya was determined to see her journey through to the end. For she knew that only by confronting the darkness that lurked within the abandoned house could she hope to uncover the truth - and perhaps, finally, find the answers she had been searching for all along.

Chapter 6: The Heart of the Forest

The abandoned house stood silent and still as Maya descended the narrow staircase, her footsteps echoing softly in the darkness. Each step brought her deeper into the unknown, her heart pounding with anticipation and apprehension.

As she reached the bottom of the staircase, Maya found herself in a vast chamber, its walls lined with ancient tapestries and mysterious carvings. Torches flickered along the stone walls, casting eerie shadows that danced across the floor.

The air was thick with the scent of dust and age, and Maya could feel the weight of centuries pressing down on her as she gazed around the chamber in awe. It was as if she had stepped into another world—a world frozen in time, waiting to be discovered.

In the center of the chamber stood a stone pedestal, upon which rested a small wooden box adorned with intricate symbols and glyphs. Maya approached it cautiously, her fingers trembling with excitement as she reached out to lift the lid.

Inside the box lay a collection of ancient artifacts—golden trinkets, jeweled amulets, and delicate scrolls bound with faded ribbon. But it was the journal nestled among the artifacts that caught Maya's eye, its leather cover worn with age but still intact.

With trembling hands, Maya lifted the journal from the box and began to read. The pages were filled with cryptic symbols and faded ink, but as she studied them, Maya felt a sense of clarity wash over her. It was as if the words were speaking directly to her, revealing secrets long hidden and truths waiting to be uncovered.

The journal spoke of a time long forgotten, when magic and mystery ruled the land. It told of a powerful artifact known as the Key of Ages—a relic of untold power that could unlock the secrets of the universe itself.

According to the journal, the Key had been hidden away by a group of ancient guardians, tasked with protecting its power from those who would seek to wield it for their own gain. But over the centuries, the guardians had disappeared, leaving behind only whispers and legends of their existence.

As Maya read on, she realized that she had stumbled upon something far greater than she had ever imagined. The abandoned house was not just a forgotten relic of the past—it was a gateway to a world of untold wonders and dangers.

But with great power came great peril, and Maya knew that she would have to tread carefully if she hoped to unlock the secrets of the Key of Ages and uncover the truth behind the mysterious doorbell.

Lost in her thoughts, Maya barely noticed as the torches along the chamber walls began to flicker and dim, casting the room into darkness. But even as the shadows closed in around her, Maya felt a sense of determination burning within her.

With the journal clutched tightly in her hand, Maya made her way back up the staircase, her mind racing with possibilities. The adventure had only just begun, and she knew that the path ahead would be fraught with challenges and obstacles.

But she was determined to see it through to the end, for she knew that the fate of not just her own world, but countless others, depended on it.

And so, with a newfound sense of purpose burning within her, Maya emerged from the hidden chamber and into the light of day, ready to face whatever lay ahead.

Chapter 7: The Guardian's Call

The morning sun cast a golden hue over the quiet streets of Willow Creek as Maya emerged from the abandoned house, her mind abuzz with a whirlwind of thoughts and emotions. The discovery of the hidden chamber had stirred something deep within her—a sense of purpose and determination that she had never experienced before.

With the journal clutched tightly in her hand, Maya made her way through the familiar streets, each step a testament to her newfound resolve. The weight of the ancient artifacts pressed against her chest, their presence a constant reminder of the journey that lay ahead.

As she walked, Maya couldn't shake the feeling that she was being watched. Shadows seemed to dance at the corner of her vision, and every rustle of leaves set her on edge. It was as if the very air around her crackled with an otherworldly energy, whispering secrets long forgotten.

Lost in thought, Maya barely noticed the passing of time as she wandered aimlessly through the streets of Willow Creek. Memories of her childhood flooded back to her—lazy summer afternoons spent exploring the woods, and cozy evenings curled up with a book by the fireplace.

But amidst the nostalgia, a sense of urgency gnawed at Maya's insides. She couldn't afford to dwell on the past, not when the fate of the world hung in the balance. There were secrets to uncover, mysteries to solve, and Maya knew that she was the only one who could unravel them.

As she reached the edge of town, Maya paused to catch her breath, the journal heavy in her hands. The sun had reached its zenith, casting harsh shadows across the landscape. In the distance, the sprawling forests of Willow Creek beckoned, their depths shrouded in mystery and intrigue.

With a determined nod, Maya set off into the woods, each step taking her further from the safety of civilization and closer to the unknown. The forest welcomed her with open arms, its ancient trees towering overhead like silent sentinels.

For hours, Maya wandered through the woods, her senses on high alert for any sign of danger. But despite her vigilance, she couldn't shake the feeling that she was being guided—drawn ever closer to her destiny by forces beyond her understanding.

As the sun began to sink below the horizon, casting long shadows across the forest floor, Maya stumbled upon a clearing bathed in moonlight. In the center of the clearing stood a circle of ancient stones, their surfaces etched with symbols and glyphs.

With a sense of reverence, Maya approached the stones, her heart pounding in her chest. There was something undeniably powerful about this place, something that resonated deep within her soul.

As she reached out to touch one of the stones, a strange sensation washed over her—a tingling warmth that spread from her fingertips to the very core of her being. In that moment, Maya knew that she was exactly where she was meant to be.

With a newfound sense of purpose burning within her, Maya opened the journal once more and began to read. Each word seemed to leap off the page, illuminating the path ahead with its ancient wisdom.

And as the night descended upon the forest, Maya knew that her journey was only just beginning.

Chapter 8: Revelations

Weeks blurred into months as Maya delved deeper into the mysteries shrouding the Key of Ages. Night after night, she poured over the ancient journal's pages, seeking clarity amidst the cryptic passages and faded ink. Each revelation brought her closer to understanding the significance of her quest, yet the true purpose of the artifact remained elusive.

In her pursuit of knowledge, Maya sought counsel from scholars and sages, delving into dusty tomes and forgotten archives in search of answers. Yet, with each dead end, frustration gnawed at her resolve, threatening to overshadow her determination.

It was during one such fruitless endeavor that Maya stumbled upon a thread of insight—a mention of Alistair the Wise, a figure steeped in legend and mystery. According to the journal, Alistair had been a custodian of the Key, entrusted with its safekeeping by the ancient guardians who had forged it.

Intrigued by the enigmatic sorcerer's role in the artifact's history, Maya embarked on a journey to uncover the truth behind his legacy. Her quest led her across distant lands and treacherous terrain, each step bringing her closer to the heart of the mystery.

Along the way, Maya encountered allies and adversaries alike, their motives as varied as the stars above. Some sought to aid her in her quest, while others sought to hinder her progress, driven by greed or fear of the unknown.

Yet, amidst the chaos and uncertainty, Maya found solace in the wisdom of Eldric, a venerable sage whose knowledge of the Key rivaled that of the ancients themselves. Under his tutelage, Maya honed her skills and expanded her understanding of the artifact's true power, preparing herself for the challenges that lay ahead.

As Maya delved deeper into Alistair's past, she uncovered a tale of sacrifice and redemption, of a man burdened by the weight of destiny and the trials of the human condition. Through his eyes, she glimpsed the true nature of the Key—a symbol of hope and renewal, capable of reshaping the very fabric of reality.

With each revelation, Maya's determination grew, fueling her resolve to unlock the secrets of the Key and fulfill her destiny as the chosen one. Though the road ahead was fraught with danger and uncertainty, she knew that she was not alone—that the power of the Key was with her, guiding her every step of the way.

DINGS N DONGS

And so, with the echoes of Alistair's legacy ringing in her ears, Maya set forth into the unknown, ready to confront whatever challenges awaited her on her journey to unlock the true potential of the Key of Ages.

Chapter 9: Lost in the Darkness

The sun dipped below the horizon, casting long shadows across the ancient ruins where Maya now found herself. The air was heavy with the weight of history, and as she stood at the threshold of the forgotten temple, a sense of anticipation gripped her heart.

According to Eldric, the next piece of the puzzle lay hidden within the temple's depths—a trial set forth by the ancient guardians to test the worthiness of those who sought the Key of Ages. With each step forward, Maya felt the weight of their gaze upon her, watching and waiting to see if she was truly worthy of their trust.

As she ventured deeper into the temple, Maya encountered a series of challenges, each more daunting than the last. From hidden traps to riddles shrouded in mystery, the guardians' tests pushed her to the limits of her abilities, forcing her to confront her fears and doubts head-on.

Yet, with each obstacle she overcame, Maya felt a surge of confidence coursing through her veins. She was not alone in this journey—the power of the Key of Ages was with her, guiding her every step of the way.

Finally, after what felt like an eternity, Maya reached the heart of the temple—a chamber bathed in the soft glow of moonlight, where the Key of Ages lay waiting, nestled atop a pedestal of stone.

With trembling hands, Maya approached the pedestal and reached out to grasp the artifact, her fingers closing around its smooth surface. In that moment, she felt a surge of power coursing through her, filling her with a sense of purpose and determination unlike anything she had ever known.

But as Maya prepared to take the Key and complete her quest, a voice echoed through the chamber—a voice that seemed to emanate from the very walls themselves.

"Halt, seeker," the voice intoned, its words reverberating in the stillness of the temple. "Before you claim the Key of Ages as your own, you must first prove yourself worthy of its power."

Maya's heart skipped a beat as she listened to the guardian's words, her mind racing with uncertainty. What test lay before her, and was she truly ready to face it?

But deep down, Maya knew that she had come too far to turn back now. With a steely resolve, she squared her shoulders and prepared to meet whatever challenge awaited her, knowing that her fate—and the fate of the world—hung in the balance.

And as the guardian's test began, Maya braced herself for the trials that lay ahead, ready to prove herself worthy of the Key of Ages and unlock its true potential once and for all.

Chapter 10: The Path Forward

The temple's depths seemed to swallow Maya whole as she descended further into its ancient halls. Shadows danced along the walls, whispering secrets long forgotten, and the air grew thick with a sense of foreboding.

As Maya pressed on, her senses heightened, every sound and movement amplified in the eerie silence. The weight of the guardian's challenge hung heavy upon her shoulders, a constant reminder of the task that lay ahead.

At last, she reached the heart of the temple—a vast chamber bathed in darkness, save for the faint flicker of torchlight that cast long, twisting shadows across the stone floor. In the center of the chamber stood a pedestal, upon which the Key of Ages gleamed faintly in the dim light.

But as Maya approached, she felt a chill run down her spine—a sense of unease that lingered in the air like a palpable presence. She knew that this was no ordinary trial, that the guardian's test would push her to her limits and beyond.

With a deep breath, Maya stepped forward, her hand outstretched towards the artifact. But before she could grasp it, the shadows around her began to shift and twist, coalescing into a swirling mass of darkness that blocked her path.

"Who dares to trespass in this sacred place?" a voice echoed through the chamber, its tone cold and menacing.

Maya's heart raced as she searched for the source of the voice, her gaze darting from shadow to shadow. "I am Maya, seeker of the Key of Ages," she replied, her voice steady despite the fear that gnawed at her insides. "I seek only to prove myself worthy of its power."

A low chuckle filled the air, sending shivers down Maya's spine. "Worthy, you say? We shall see about that," the voice replied, its tone dripping with malice.

And with that, the shadows surged forward, enveloping Maya in darkness. She stumbled backward, her heart pounding in her chest as she fought to regain her bearings.

But as she struggled against the suffocating darkness, a voice whispered in her mind—a voice that was not her own, but that of the Key of Ages itself.

"Trust in yourself, Maya," the voice urged, its words a beacon of light in the midst of the darkness. "You are stronger than you know."

With renewed determination, Maya pushed back against the shadows, her hands glowing with an inner light. Slowly but surely, she began to drive back the darkness, inch by inch, until at last, the chamber was bathed in light once more.

And there, standing before her, was the guardian of the temple—a figure cloaked in shadows, yet with eyes that burned bright with ancient wisdom.

"You have passed the trial of shadows, Maya," the guardian intoned, its voice filled with respect. "You have proven yourself worthy of the Key of Ages."

With a sense of relief flooding through her, Maya reached out and grasped the artifact, feeling its power surge through her veins. In that moment, she knew that her journey was far from over—but with the Key of Ages by her side, she was ready to face whatever trials lay ahead.

Chapter 11: Secrets Revealed

As Maya emerged from the depths of the ancient temple, the weight of the guardian's challenge still hung heavy on her mind. The trials she had faced had tested her strength and resolve like never before, leaving her shaken but determined to press onward.

With the Key of Ages safely in her possession, Maya made her way back to the world above, her footsteps echoing in the cavernous halls of the temple. The air felt charged with anticipation, as if the very earth itself awaited her next move.

But as Maya stepped out into the fading light of day, she was greeted by a sight that sent a chill down her spine—a figure cloaked in shadow, lurking at the edge of the temple's entrance.

Instinctively, Maya reached for the hilt of her sword, her senses on high alert as she prepared to defend herself against this new threat. But as the figure stepped forward into the light,

Maya's breath caught in her throat—it was Eldric, the sage who had guided her on her journey thus far.

Relief washed over Maya as she realized that she was not alone, but her relief was short-lived as Eldric's expression darkened with concern.

"Maya," he said gravely, his voice barely above a whisper. "There is something you must know."

As Eldric spoke, Maya listened intently, her heart sinking with each word. He spoke of a darkness that threatened to consume the world, a shadowy force that sought to wield the power of the Key of Ages for its own nefarious purposes.

But worst of all, Eldric spoke of betrayal—a betrayal from within their own ranks, from someone Maya had trusted implicitly.

As the weight of Eldric's words settled over her, Maya felt a surge of doubt and uncertainty gnawing at her resolve. Could it be true? Could someone she had considered a friend and ally truly be working against her?

But deep down, Maya knew that she could not afford to let doubt cloud her judgment. The fate of the world hung in the balance, and she alone held the key to stopping the darkness that threatened to consume it.

With a steely resolve, Maya squared her shoulders and turned to face the path ahead. She may not know what lay in store for her, but one thing was certain—she would stop at nothing to protect the Key of Ages and ensure that it did not fall into the wrong hands.

And with Eldric by her side, Maya set out once more, ready to confront whatever challenges awaited her on her journey to save the world from the shadows that lurked within.

Chapter 12: A Glimmer of Hope

The night was quiet as Maya wandered the cobblestone streets of the ancient city, her mind awash with thoughts of the guardian's test and the doubts that lingered within her. The soft glow of lanterns cast long shadows across the narrow alleys, illuminating the path ahead as Maya sought solace in the embrace of the city's ancient walls.

As she walked, Maya couldn't shake the feeling that she was being watched, the hairs on the back of her neck prickling with unease. It was as if a presence lingered just beyond the edge of her senses, whispering secrets in the darkness.

Turning a corner, Maya found herself face to face with a hooded figure, their features obscured by the shadows. Instinctively, Maya reached for the hilt of her sword, her heart pounding in her chest as she braced herself for danger.

But as the figure stepped forward into the flickering light of a nearby lantern, Maya's fears melted away, replaced by a sense of recognition. It was Susej, the mysterious man who had crossed her path time and time again on her journey.

"Susej," Maya said, her voice a mixture of surprise and curiosity. "What are you doing here?"

The hooded figure regarded Maya with an enigmatic smile, his eyes gleaming with hidden knowledge. "I have been following your journey, Maya," he said cryptically. "And I believe that our paths are intertwined in ways you cannot yet understand."

Maya's brow furrowed in confusion. "What do you mean?" she asked, her voice tinged with suspicion.

But before Susej could answer, a sudden gust of wind swept through the alley, carrying with it the faint echo of distant whispers. Maya's senses tingled as she strained to make out the words, her heart pounding in her chest as she felt the weight of destiny pressing down upon her.

"Susej," Maya said, turning to face the mysterious man once more. "What do you know about the Key of Ages? And why do I feel like there's more to our connection than meets the eye?"

Susej's smile widened, his eyes twinkling with amusement. "All will be revealed in time, Maya," he said cryptically. "But for now, trust in yourself and the path that lies ahead. The whispers of fate will guide you if you only listen."

With that, Susej disappeared into the shadows, leaving Maya alone with her thoughts once more. As she pondered his words, Maya felt a sense of clarity wash over her, banishing the doubts that had clouded her mind.

With a renewed sense of purpose, Maya set off into the night, her heart filled with determination to uncover the secrets of the Key of Ages and unravel the mysteries that lay ahead in her journey.

Chapter 13: The Darkening Sky

The night stretched its tendrils over the sleepy town of Millgrove, casting shadows that danced in the flickering glow of streetlights. Maya sat alone in her dimly lit study, the soft glow of her desk lamp casting long shadows across the worn pages of the ancient journal.

As she traced her fingers over the faded ink, Maya's mind buzzed with a cacophony of thoughts and questions. The events of the past few days had left her shaken, the weight of her newfound responsibilities pressing down upon her like a leaden cloak.

But amidst the chaos of her thoughts, Maya sensed something stirring in the shadows—a whisper, barely audible yet unmistakably present. She glanced around the room, her heart pounding in her chest as she strained to catch any sign of movement.

"Who's there?" Maya called out, her voice echoing in the silence of the room.

But there was no response, only the faint rustle of the curtains as a gentle breeze swept through the open window. Maya shivered, a chill creeping down her spine as she turned back to the journal on her desk.

With trembling hands, Maya opened the pages of the ancient tome, her eyes scanning the text for any clue that might shed light on the mysterious presence lurking in the darkness. But as she read, the words seemed to blur and twist before her eyes, their meaning eluding her grasp.

Frustration bubbled up inside Maya, mingling with the fear that gnawed at her from within. She had come too far to be deterred by mere shadows, yet the sense of unease that hung in the air was undeniable.

As the night wore on, Maya continued her vigil, her senses heightened as she strained to catch any sign of the mysterious presence that lurked in the darkness. But try as she might, there was no trace of the intruder, only the oppressive weight of the night pressing down upon her like a suffocating blanket.

Hours passed in tense silence, until finally, as the first light of dawn began to filter through the curtains, Maya felt a sense of relief wash over her. The night had passed without incident, and though the sense of unease still lingered, Maya knew that she had weathered the storm.

With a weary sigh, Maya closed the ancient journal and rose from her desk, the weight of exhaustion settling over her like a heavy cloak. As she made her way to bed, she couldn't shake the feeling that the shadows held secrets yet to be revealed, whispering their dark mysteries in the depths of the night.

And as Maya drifted off to sleep, the whispers of the shadows followed her into the realm of dreams, their elusive secrets tantalizingly out of reach.

Chapter 14: A Journey's End

As the sun dipped below the horizon, casting a golden hue over the tranquil town of Millgrove, Maya found herself drawn once again to the dusty confines of the town archives. The ancient building loomed before her, its weathered façade a testament to the passage of time.

With each step she took, Maya felt a sense of anticipation building within her. The archives held the key to unlocking the secrets of Millgrove's past, and Maya was determined to uncover the truth hidden within its walls.

Pushing open the creaking door, Maya stepped into the dimly lit interior of the archives, the scent of old paper and dust filling her nostrils. Rows upon rows of shelves lined the room, each one filled with volumes of history waiting to be discovered.

With a sense of purpose, Maya began her search, her fingers trailing over the spines of ancient tomes as she scanned the titles for any mention of the Key of Ages. Hours passed in a blur as Maya lost herself in the pages of history, each revelation bringing her closer to the truth she sought.

And then, as if guided by an unseen hand, Maya's gaze fell upon a faded manuscript tucked away in a forgotten corner of the archives. With trembling hands, she pulled the dusty tome from its resting place, her heart pounding in her chest as she flipped through its pages.

As she read, Maya's eyes widened in astonishment, for the manuscript spoke of a time long forgotten—a time when the Key of Ages had played a pivotal role in the fate of Millgrove and its inhabitants. According to the ancient text, the artifact had been wielded by a powerful sorcerer known as Alistair the Wise, who had used its power to protect the town from unspeakable darkness.

But as Maya delved deeper into the manuscript, she uncovered a darker truth lurking beneath the surface. It spoke of betrayal and corruption, of a shadowy figure who had sought to harness the power of the Key for their own nefarious purposes, threatening to plunge Millgrove into eternal darkness.

With each revelation, Maya's determination grew, fueled by the knowledge that the fate of her town rested in her hands. Armed with the newfound insight gleaned from the archives, Maya vowed to uncover the truth behind the Key of Ages and put an end to the darkness that threatened to consume Millgrove once and for all.

As she stepped out into the cool night air, Maya felt a sense of purpose coursing through her veins. The journey ahead would not be easy, but she knew that she was not alone. With the echoes of the past guiding her way, Maya set forth into the night, ready to face whatever challenges lay ahead in her quest for truth and justice.

Chapter 15: The Forest's Embrace

As the moon rose high in the night sky, casting its ethereal glow over the quiet streets of Millgrove, Maya found herself ensnared in a web of deception that threatened to unravel the very fabric of her reality. With each passing moment, the darkness seemed to press in on her from all sides, suffocating her with its malevolent presence.

Haunted by the revelations she had uncovered in the town archives, Maya knew that she was running out of time. The shadows that lurked in the corners of her vision whispered of impending doom, their sinister voices echoing in her mind like a chorus of lost souls.

Desperate for answers, Maya sought solace in the only place she knew she could find them—the home of Eldric, the sage who had guided her on her journey thus far. With a sense of urgency gnawing at her heart, Maya made her way through the deserted streets, her footsteps echoing in the stillness of the night.

As she reached Eldric's doorstep, Maya pounded on the door with trembling hands, her breath coming in ragged gasps. To her relief, the door swung open, revealing the sage standing before her with a concerned expression on his face.

"Maya, what brings you here at this hour?" Eldric asked, his voice filled with concern.

"I need your help, Eldric," Maya replied, her voice barely above a whisper. "The darkness... it's closing in on me. I don't know how much longer I can hold on."

Eldric's brow furrowed in concern as he ushered Maya inside, closing the door behind her with a resounding thud. "Tell me everything," he urged, his eyes searching Maya's face for any sign of deception.

And so, Maya recounted her journey—the trials she had faced, the secrets she had uncovered, and the darkness that threatened to consume her soul. With each word she spoke, the weight of her burden lifted ever so slightly, until finally, she felt as though she could breathe again.

But as Maya finished her tale, a shadow passed over Eldric's face, his expression darkening with concern. "The darkness you speak of, Maya... it is more insidious than you realize," he said gravely. "There are forces at work here that seek to manipulate and deceive us at every turn."

Maya's heart sank at Eldric's words, the weight of his warning settling over her like a shroud. "What can we do?" she asked, her voice trembling with fear.

Eldric placed a comforting hand on Maya's shoulder, his touch grounding her in the present moment. "We must tread carefully, Maya, for the path ahead is fraught with danger," he said solemnly. "But fear not, for as long as we stand together, we can overcome any obstacle that lies in our path."

With Eldric's words ringing in her ears, Maya felt a renewed sense of determination coursing through her veins. The darkness may have surrounded her, but she refused to let it consume her. With Eldric by her side, Maya knew that she had the strength to face whatever challenges lay ahead, no matter how daunting they may seem.

And so, as the night wore on and the moon cast its silvery light over the sleeping town of Millgrove, Maya and Eldric prepared themselves for the battle that lay ahead—a battle against the darkness that threatened to engulf them both in its icy embrace.

Chapter 16: Beyond the Veil

The moon hung low in the night sky, casting its silvery glow over the quiet streets of Millgrove. Maya walked alone through the deserted town, her footsteps echoing softly against the cobblestone pavement. As she made her way towards the outskirts of town, a sense of unease settled over her like a heavy shroud.

Ever since her discovery in the archives, Maya had been plagued by a nagging suspicion—a feeling that there was more to the story than met the eye. The revelations about Alistair the Wise and the ancient sorcery that had once protected Millgrove seemed too convenient, too neatly packaged to be the whole truth.

As she approached the edge of the forest that bordered the town, Maya's senses went on high alert. The air seemed to hum with an otherworldly energy, and a chill wind whispered through the trees, carrying with it a sense of foreboding.

Steeling herself against the rising tide of fear, Maya pressed on, determined to uncover the truth hidden within the shadows. With each step she took, the forest grew darker and denser, the trees looming like silent sentinels in the night.

Suddenly, a rustling in the underbrush caught Maya's attention, and she froze, her heart pounding in her chest. Peering into the darkness, she strained to catch a glimpse of whatever lurked within the shadows.

And then, emerging from the depths of the forest, came a figure—a silhouette cloaked in darkness, its features obscured by the veil of night. Maya's breath caught in her throat as she watched the figure draw closer, a sense of dread settling over her like a suffocating fog.

"Who goes there?" Maya called out, her voice trembling with fear.

The figure stopped in its tracks, its gaze fixed on Maya with an intensity that sent shivers down her spine. And then, to Maya's horror, the figure spoke—a voice as cold and chilling as the winter wind.

"You seek the truth, little one," the figure intoned, its words sending a shiver down Maya's spine. "But be warned—truth is a double-edged sword, capable of revealing as much as it conceals."

Maya's mind raced with a thousand questions, but before she could speak, the figure vanished into the darkness, leaving Maya alone once more with her thoughts.

As she stood there in the eerie stillness of the forest, Maya knew that she was standing at the precipice of something far greater than herself. The veil of deception had been lifted, revealing a world of darkness and danger lurking just beyond the surface.

With a sense of determination burning in her heart, Maya vowed to press on, no matter the cost. For she knew that the truth awaited her in the shadows, and she would stop at nothing to uncover it.

Chapter 17: The Unseen Truth

The ancient trees of the forest loomed overhead, their gnarled branches reaching towards the night sky like twisted fingers clawing at the heavens. Maya moved cautiously through the dense undergrowth, her senses alert for any sign of danger.

As she ventured deeper into the heart of the forest, Maya felt a sense of reverence wash over her—a feeling of being in the presence of something ancient and powerful. The air thrummed with an otherworldly energy, and Maya couldn't shake the feeling that she was being watched by unseen eyes.

Suddenly, a soft whisper floated through the trees, barely audible yet unmistakably present. Maya froze in her tracks, her heart pounding in her chest as she strained to catch the sound.

"Seeker of truth," the whisper seemed to say, its voice echoing in Maya's mind like a distant memory. "Beware the shadows that lurk within the depths of the forest, for they hold secrets long forgotten."

Maya's pulse quickened at the words, a chill running down her spine. She knew that she was treading on dangerous ground, but the lure of the truth beckoned her ever onward.

With each step she took, the whispers grew louder, a cacophony of voices speaking in languages long lost to time. Maya closed her eyes, allowing the ancient words to wash over her, their meaning elusive yet tantalizingly close.

And then, as if guided by an unseen hand, Maya found herself standing before a towering monolith hidden deep within the heart of the forest. The ancient stone seemed to pulse with a faint glow, its surface etched with intricate symbols and glyphs.

With trembling hands, Maya reached out to touch the monolith, her fingertips tracing the ancient runes with reverence. As she did, a surge of power coursed through her, filling her with a sense of clarity and purpose.

In that moment, Maya understood. The forest was alive with the echoes of the ancients, their whispers carrying the wisdom of generations past. And she, as the seeker of truth, held the key to unlocking their secrets.

With newfound resolve, Maya closed her eyes and allowed herself to be enveloped by the whispers of the ancients, their words guiding her on her journey towards enlightenment.

Chapter 18: Into the Depths

As Maya ventured deeper into the heart of the forest, the trees seemed to close in around her, their branches intertwining like skeletal fingers grasping at the darkness. The air grew thick with the scent of earth and moss, and a sense of unease settled over Maya like a heavy cloak.

With each step she took, the shadows seemed to deepen, twisting and shifting in the dim light of the moon. Maya felt as though she were being watched, the sensation of eyes boring into her from all sides sending shivers down her spine.

But Maya pressed on, her determination unwavering in the face of the unknown. She had come too far to turn back now, and the truth she sought lay just beyond her grasp.

Suddenly, a rustling in the underbrush caught Maya's attention, and she froze, her heart pounding in her chest. Peering into the darkness, she strained to catch a glimpse of whatever lurked within the shadows.

And then, emerging from the depths of the forest, came a figure—a silhouette cloaked in darkness, its features obscured by the veil of night. Maya's breath caught in her throat as she watched the figure draw closer, a sense of dread settling over her like a suffocating fog.

"Who goes there?" Maya called out, her voice trembling with fear.

The figure stopped in its tracks, its gaze fixed on Maya with an intensity that sent shivers down her spine. And then, to Maya's horror, the figure spoke—a voice as cold and chilling as the winter wind.

"You seek the truth, little one," the figure intoned, its words sending a shiver down Maya's spine. "But be warned—truth is a double-edged sword, capable of revealing as much as it conceals."

Maya's mind raced with a thousand questions, but before she could speak, the figure vanished into the darkness, leaving Maya alone once more with her thoughts.

As she stood there in the eerie stillness of the forest, Maya knew that she was standing at the precipice of something far greater than herself. The veil of deception had been lifted, revealing a world of darkness and danger lurking just beyond the surface.

With a sense of determination burning in her heart, Maya vowed to press on, no matter the cost. For she knew that the truth awaited her in the shadows, and she would stop at nothing to uncover it.

Chapter 19: The Heart of Darkness

As Maya ventured deeper into the heart of the forest, the air grew thick with a palpable sense of foreboding. Every rustle of the leaves, every whisper of the wind seemed to echo with a sinister intent, sending a shiver down Maya's spine.

She knew she was close now—close to uncovering the truth that had eluded her for so long. But with each step she took, the path ahead seemed to grow darker, more treacherous, as if the forest itself conspired to keep its secrets hidden.

The trees loomed overhead like silent sentinels, their twisted branches casting long, twisted shadows that danced in the flickering light of the moon. Maya moved cautiously through the undergrowth, her senses on high alert for any sign of danger.

And then, just when Maya thought she could go no further, she stumbled upon it—a clearing bathed in an eerie, otherworldly glow. At its center stood a towering stone pedestal, upon which rested a single, ornate key—the Key of Ages.

Maya's heart pounded in her chest as she approached the pedestal, her eyes fixed on the ancient artifact before her. She reached out a trembling hand, her fingers brushing against the cool, smooth surface of the key.

But as Maya's hand closed around the artifact, a sudden surge of power coursed through her, sending her reeling backwards. She cried out in pain as visions flashed before her eyes—visions of darkness and despair, of ancient evils stirring in the depths of the forest.

And then, just as suddenly as it had begun, the visions ceased, leaving Maya gasping for breath on the forest floor. She staggered to her feet, her mind reeling with the enormity of what she had just experienced.

With trembling hands, Maya retrieved the Key of Ages from where it lay, clutching it tightly to her chest. She knew now that she held the key to unlocking the truth, to unraveling the mysteries that had haunted her for so long.

But as Maya turned to leave the clearing, a voice echoed in her mind—a voice both ancient and familiar, speaking words of warning and prophecy.

"Beware, seeker of truth," the voice intoned. "For the darkness you seek to vanquish may yet consume you whole."

Maya's heart sank at the words, but she knew that she could not turn back now. With the Key of Ages in her possession, she was closer than ever to uncovering the truth behind the ancient sorcery that had plagued her town for centuries.

DINGS N DONGS

With a steely resolve, Maya set forth into the heart of darkness, her path illuminated by the light of the moon and the unwavering determination burning in her heart.

Chapter 20: A Light in the Darkness

With the Key of Ages clutched tightly in her grasp, Maya felt a renewed sense of purpose coursing through her veins. The weight of the ancient artifact pressed against her chest, a tangible reminder of the journey she had undertaken and the truths she sought to uncover.

As she made her way back through the forest, Maya's mind raced with questions. What secrets did the Key hold? What darkness lurked within the shadows, waiting to be revealed? And most importantly, how would Maya confront the truth once she found it?

The forest seemed to come alive around her, the rustle of the leaves and the whisper of the wind echoing like a chorus of voices urging her onward. Maya followed the path she had carved through the undergrowth, her footsteps steady and sure despite the uncertainty that lay ahead.

As she emerged from the depths of the forest, Maya found herself standing once again on the outskirts of Millgrove. The town lay before her, bathed in the soft light of dawn, its streets empty and silent in the early morning hours.

But Maya knew that the calm belied the storm that brewed beneath the surface. The darkness that had plagued Millgrove for so long was still present, lurking just beyond the reach of the light.

With a sense of determination burning in her heart, Maya made her way through the deserted streets, the Key of Ages pulsing with energy in her hand. She knew that she could not face the darkness alone, but she also knew that she had allies—friends who would stand by her side no matter what.

As Maya approached the town square, she saw them waiting for her—a small group of brave souls who had pledged themselves to her cause. Their faces were grim, their eyes filled with determination as they prepared to face the darkness head-on.

With a silent nod of gratitude, Maya joined her friends, the Key of Ages glowing brightly in her hand. Together, they stood on the threshold of a new dawn, ready to confront the truth and unravel the mysteries that had plagued their town for centuries.

And as the first rays of sunlight broke over the horizon, Maya knew that no matter what trials lay ahead, they would face them together—as friends, as allies, and as champions of the light.

Chapter 21: The Final Revelation

The town square stood silent and empty, bathed in the soft glow of the moon overhead. Maya and her companions gathered in a circle, their faces illuminated by the pale light as they prepared to embark on their journey into the heart of the forest.

The Key of Ages, cradled in Maya's hand, pulsed with a faint, ethereal light—a beacon of hope in the encroaching darkness. But despite the reassurance it offered, doubts still lingered in the minds of Maya and her allies. The path ahead was fraught with peril, and the mysteries of Millgrove ran deeper than any of them had imagined.

As they stood in silence, a sudden gust of wind swept through the square, carrying with it the faint echoes of whispers from the past. Maya strained to make out the words, her senses tingling with anticipation as the voices danced on the edge of her consciousness.

"It's the spirits of the forest," whispered one of Maya's companions, their voice barely audible above the wind. "They seek to guide us on our journey."

With a sense of reverence, Maya closed her eyes and reached out with her mind, allowing the voices to wash over her like a river of memories. Visions flashed before her eyes—scenes from a time long forgotten, when the forest was teeming with life and the land was ruled by ancient powers.

She saw the towering trees swaying in the breeze, their branches reaching towards the heavens in silent supplication. She saw the creatures of the forest—mysterious and elusive—darting through the undergrowth with grace and agility. And she saw the spirits of the ancestors, their presence felt in every rustle of the leaves and every whisper of the wind.

But amidst the beauty of the past, Maya also saw glimpses of darkness—a shadowy figure lurking in the shadows, its eyes filled with malice and its heart consumed by greed. She felt a chill run down her spine as the figure drew closer, its presence casting a pall over the once vibrant landscape.

As the visions faded and Maya opened her eyes, she felt a newfound resolve stirring within her. The journey ahead would not be easy, but she knew that they could not turn back now. The fate of Millgrove—and perhaps even the fate of the forest itself—rested in their hands.

With a silent nod to her companions, Maya took a deep breath and stepped forward, the Key of Ages glowing brightly in her hand. The time had come to face their destiny—to unlock the secrets of the past and forge a new future for themselves and their town.

And as they set out into the forest once more, Maya couldn't help but feel a glimmer of hope amidst the encroaching darkness. For she knew that as long as they stood together, they would never be truly alone.

Chapter 22: The Edge of Darkness

The forest grew dense around Maya and her companions, the tangled undergrowth muffling their footsteps as they pressed forward. Shadows danced between the trees, and the air hung heavy with an ominous stillness.

"I don't like this," whispered one of Maya's companions, their voice barely audible over the rustle of leaves. "It feels like we're being watched."

Maya nodded, her senses on high alert as they navigated the winding path ahead. "Stay close," she urged, her grip tightening on the Key of Ages. "We need to stick together."

But despite their efforts to remain vigilant, the forest seemed to conspire against them. Whispers drifted through the trees, soft and insistent, teasing at the edges of their consciousness.

"Do you hear that?" Maya whispered, her heart pounding in her chest as she strained to make out the words.

Her companions nodded, their expressions tense with apprehension. "It sounds like... voices," one of them replied, their voice barely more than a breath.

As they ventured deeper into the forest, the whispers grew louder, their words twisting and distorting in the darkness. Maya clenched her jaw, her resolve hardening with each step. They had come too far to turn back now, not when the truth lay just beyond their grasp.

Suddenly, the forest fell silent, the oppressive stillness weighing heavily upon them. Maya exchanged a wary glance with her companions, their eyes reflecting the same mixture of fear and determination that burned within her own.

"We're getting close," Maya murmured, her voice barely audible over the hush of the trees. "I can feel it."

But before they could take another step, a voice pierced the silence—a soft, haunting whisper that seemed to emanate from the very depths of the forest itself.

"You seek answers," it murmured, its words echoing through the trees like a siren's call. "But the truth you seek may be more than you can bear."

Maya's grip tightened on the Key of Ages, her resolve unwavering despite the chill that crept up her spine. "We'll take our chances," she replied, her voice steady with determination. "Whatever awaits us, we'll face it together."

With a shared nod of understanding, Maya and her companions pressed on, their footsteps echoing through the silent forest as they ventured ever deeper into the heart of darkness.

Chapter 23: The Journey's Conclusion

As Maya and her companions ventured deeper into the heart of the forest, the darkness seemed to envelop them like a suffocating shroud. The towering trees loomed overhead, their branches casting eerie shadows that danced across the forest floor.

"I don't like this," whispered Maya, her voice barely audible over the rustle of leaves. "It feels as though the forest itself is closing in around us."

Her companions nodded in silent agreement, their eyes scanning the shadows for any sign of movement. But despite their unease, they pressed forward, their determination unwavering in the face of the unknown.

As they traversed the winding path, the air grew thick with tension, each step weighed down by the oppressive weight of the forest's silence. It was as though the very essence of the forest had turned against them, its ancient secrets lurking just beyond their reach.

Suddenly, a voice broke through the stillness—a soft, melodic whisper that sent shivers down Maya's spine. She turned to her companions, but they too had heard it, their eyes wide with fear.

"What was that?" one of them asked, their voice trembling with apprehension.

Maya shook her head, her senses on high alert as she strained to make out the words. "I'm not sure," she replied, her voice barely more than a whisper. "But we need to keep moving. We're getting closer to the truth."

With a shared nod of understanding, Maya and her companions pressed on, their footsteps echoing through the silent forest as they ventured ever deeper into the unknown.

But as they rounded a bend in the path, they were met with a sight that sent chills down their spines—a clearing bathed in an otherworldly glow, its edges blurred by a veil of shadows that seemed to pulse with a life of their own.

In the center of the clearing stood a figure cloaked in darkness, its eyes gleaming with malevolence as it watched Maya and her companions approach.

"You have come seeking answers," it intoned, its voice echoing through the clearing like a bell tolling in the night. "But the truth you seek may be more than you can bear."

Maya squared her shoulders, her grip tightening on the Key of Ages as she prepared to face whatever lay ahead. "We'll take our chances," she replied, her voice steady with determination. "No matter what awaits us, we'll face it together."

With a silent nod of agreement, Maya and her companions stepped forward, ready to confront the darkness and uncover the secrets that lay hidden within the heart of the forest.

Chapter 24: The Final Confrontation

As Maya and her companions stood on the threshold of the glowing clearing, the air seemed to crackle with an otherworldly energy. The veil of shadows that surrounded them pulsed with an eerie light, casting strange patterns upon the forest floor.

"We're close now," Maya murmured, her voice barely audible over the whispering wind. "I can feel it."

Her companions nodded in silent agreement, their eyes fixed on the figure in the center of the clearing—a dark silhouette against the pulsing light. It seemed to beckon them forward, its presence both mesmerizing and foreboding.

With a shared breath, Maya and her companions stepped into the clearing, their senses tingling with anticipation. The ground beneath their feet felt alive with power, humming with the echoes of ancient magic.

As they approached the figure, it spoke—a voice like thunder echoing through the clearing, filling Maya's mind with images of a time long past.

"You have come seeking the truth," it intoned, its words reverberating through the air like a solemn oath. "But the path you tread is fraught with danger."

Maya squared her shoulders, her resolve unwavering in the face of the unknown. "We know the risks," she replied, her voice steady with determination. "But we will not turn back now."

The figure regarded them with an inscrutable gaze, its eyes burning with a fierce intensity. "Very well," it said, its voice a low rumble that seemed to shake the very ground beneath their feet. "But know this—what you seek may not be what you find."

With that, the figure vanished, leaving Maya and her companions standing alone in the clearing, the echoes of its words lingering in the air like a haunting melody.

"We need to be cautious," Maya said, her voice barely above a whisper. "Whatever awaits us, we must be prepared."

Her companions nodded in agreement, their eyes scanning the clearing for any sign of danger. But as they stepped forward, the ground beneath them began to tremble, and the air grew thick with a sense of impending doom.

With a shared breath, Maya and her companions steeled themselves for whatever lay ahead, knowing that their journey was far from over.

Chapter 25: The Last Stand

As Maya and her companions pressed deeper into the heart of the forest, a sense of foreboding hung heavy in the air. The trees seemed to lean in closer, their branches twisted and gnarled like the fingers of some ancient guardian.

"We're getting closer," Maya murmured, her voice barely audible over the rustle of leaves. "I can feel it."

Her companions nodded in agreement, their eyes scanning the shadows for any sign of movement. But despite their vigilance, the forest remained eerily silent, as though holding its breath in anticipation.

Suddenly, they came upon a clearing bathed in dappled sunlight, its edges blurred by the shifting shadows that danced across the forest floor. At the center of the clearing stood a solitary figure—a towering statue carved from stone, its features weathered by centuries of exposure to the elements.

"What is that?" one of Maya's companions whispered, their voice filled with awe.

Maya approached the statue cautiously, her eyes scanning its weathered features for any sign of life. But as she drew closer, she realized that there was more to the statue than met the eye. Etched into its base were a series of ancient runes, their meaning lost to time.

"It's a riddle," Maya said, her voice filled with wonder. "A challenge left behind by those who came before us."

With trembling fingers, Maya traced the runes, her mind racing as she tried to decipher their meaning. But the more she studied them, the more they seemed to elude her grasp, twisting and turning like the branches of the forest itself.

"We need to solve this riddle," Maya said, her voice determined. "It could hold the key to unlocking the secrets of the forest."

Her companions nodded in agreement, their eyes alight with excitement. Together, they set to work, pouring over the runes and debating their possible meanings.

Hours passed as they wrestled with the riddle, their frustration mounting with each passing moment. But just as they were about to give up hope, Maya's gaze fell upon a series of symbols that seemed to form a pattern—a pattern that held the key to unlocking the riddle's secrets.

"It's a map," Maya exclaimed, her voice filled with triumph. "A map that will lead us to the heart of the forest."

With renewed determination, Maya and her companions set out into the depths of the forest, following the clues laid out before them. And as they ventured deeper into the shadows, they knew that their journey was far from over. But with the riddle solved and the path clear, they were one step closer to uncovering the truth that lay hidden within the heart of the forest.

Chapter 26: Through the Shadows

As Maya and her companions ventured deeper into the heart of the forest, the air grew thick with anticipation. Each step brought them closer to the answers they sought, yet the shadows seemed to stretch endlessly before them, weaving tales of forgotten whispers and ancient mysteries.

"We're nearing the heart of the forest," Maya said, her voice tinged with excitement. "Stay alert."

Her companions nodded in agreement, their eyes scanning the surrounding trees for any sign of movement. The forest exhaled a hushed silence, broken only by the whisper of leaves and the soft crunch of fallen twigs beneath their feet.

Suddenly, they stumbled upon a clearing bathed in moonlight, its ethereal glow casting strange shadows upon the forest floor. At the center of the clearing stood a towering tree, its branches reaching towards the sky like fingers grasping for the heavens.

"This must be it," Maya whispered, her voice barely more than a breath.

As they approached the tree, they noticed strange markings etched into its bark—symbols that seemed to pulse with an otherworldly energy, as if imbued with the ancient wisdom of the forest itself. Maya reached out to touch the markings, her fingers tingling with anticipation.

"It's like nothing I've ever seen," one of Maya's companions remarked, their voice filled with wonder.

But as Maya traced the symbols, a strange sensation washed over her—a feeling of familiarity mixed with a creeping sense of unease. Memories flashed through her mind, fragments of a past long forgotten, and she realized that the tree held secrets that went far beyond anything they could have imagined.

"We need to keep moving," Maya said, her voice determined. "There's something deeper within the forest that we need to find."

With a shared nod of understanding, Maya and her companions continued on their journey, their hearts filled with a sense of purpose. For they knew that the answers they sought lay just beyond the shadows, waiting to be discovered in the hidden depths of the ancient forest.

Chapter 27: The Veil Unraveled

As Maya and her companions delved deeper into the heart of the forest, the air grew heavy with anticipation, each breath tinged with the scent of earth and ancient magic. Shadows danced among the trees, weaving tales of forgotten whispers and hidden truths.

"We're getting closer," Maya murmured, her voice barely more than a whisper. "I can feel it in my bones."

Her companions nodded in agreement, their eyes darting nervously to the shifting shadows that surrounded them. The forest seemed to pulse with an otherworldly energy, its secrets tantalizingly close yet maddeningly out of reach.

Suddenly, they stumbled upon a clearing bathed in silvery moonlight, its ethereal glow illuminating the forest floor with an otherworldly radiance. At the center of the clearing stood a circle of ancient stones, their weathered surfaces bearing the weight of countless centuries.

"This is it," Maya breathed, her heart pounding with excitement.

As they approached the circle, they noticed strange symbols etched into the stones—symbols that seemed to writhe and twist with a life of their own. Maya reached out to touch the nearest stone, her fingers tracing the intricate patterns with a sense of awe and reverence.

"These are the symbols of the ancients," one of Maya's companions whispered, their voice filled with wonder. "They speak of a time long forgotten, when the forest was alive with magic and mystery."

But as Maya studied the symbols, she sensed something stirring in the air—a presence lurking just beyond the edge of her awareness. She glanced nervously at her companions, but they too seemed to sense the shifting currents of the forest, their eyes wide with trepidation.

"We're not alone," Maya whispered, her voice barely more than a breath.

With a shared nod of understanding, Maya and her companions braced themselves for whatever lay ahead. For they knew that the forest held secrets far older and more powerful than they could ever have imagined, and they were determined to uncover the truth, no matter the cost.

Chapter 28: A Whisper in the Wind

As Maya and her companions pressed deeper into the heart of the forest, a sense of unease settled over them like a shroud. The trees loomed overhead, their branches twisted and gnarled like the fingers of some ancient guardian, casting long shadows that seemed to reach out and ensnare them.

"We're nearing the heart of the darkness," Maya whispered, her voice barely audible over the rustle of leaves.

Her companions nodded in silent agreement, their eyes scanning the surrounding shadows for any sign of movement. The forest seemed to hold its breath, as though waiting for the moment to reveal its secrets.

Suddenly, they stumbled upon a clearing shrouded in darkness, its edges blurred by the shifting shadows that danced across the forest floor. At the center of the clearing stood a towering figure—a silhouette cloaked in darkness, its features obscured by the veil of night.

"What is that?" one of Maya's companions whispered, their voice filled with fear.

But as they approached the figure, they realized that it was not a figure at all, but a tree—a tree unlike any they had ever seen. Its branches twisted and contorted like the limbs of some monstrous creature, its leaves whispering secrets lost to time.

"It's the Veil of Shadows," Maya murmured, her voice heavy with dread. "A barrier between the world of the living and the realm of the dead."

Her companions glanced nervously at one another, their faces pale with fear. They knew that to pass through the Veil of Shadows was to risk their very souls, yet they also knew that their journey could not end here.

"We must press on," Maya said, her voice firm. "There are answers waiting for us on the other side, and we cannot turn back now."

With a shared nod of understanding, Maya and her companions stepped forward, their hearts pounding with fear and anticipation. For beyond the Veil of Shadows lay the heart of the darkness, and the truth that they had been seeking all along.

Chapter 29: The Final Revelation

As Maya and her companions stood before the Veil of Shadows, a sense of anticipation hung heavy in the air. The darkness seemed to pulse with a malevolent energy, whispering secrets that sent shivers down their spines.

"We've come too far to turn back now," Maya said, her voice firm despite the fear gnawing at her heart.

Her companions nodded in agreement, their faces set with determination. They knew that whatever lay beyond the Veil of Shadows would test their courage and resolve like never before.

With a deep breath, Maya stepped forward, her hand outstretched towards the darkness. As her fingers brushed against the barrier, a surge of power coursed through her, sending sparks of light dancing along her skin.

The Veil rippled like water, parting before Maya's touch to reveal a world unlike any they had ever seen. Shadows danced and flickered, twisting into strange shapes that seemed to beckon them forward.

"We must be cautious," one of Maya's companions warned, their voice barely more than a whisper. "There's no telling what dangers lie beyond."

But Maya pressed on, her determination unyielding. She knew that they were close now, closer than they had ever been to uncovering the truth that had eluded them for so long.

As they stepped through the Veil of Shadows, the world around them shifted and changed, morphing into a landscape of darkness and despair. But Maya was undeterred, her eyes fixed on the horizon where a single point of light burned bright against the darkness.

"We're almost there," Maya said, her voice filled with determination. "The answers we seek are within reach."

With renewed purpose, Maya and her companions pressed forward, their hearts filled with hope and anticipation. For they knew that beyond the darkness lay the final revelation—a truth that would change their lives forever.

Chapter 30: The Unveiling

The air hung heavy with anticipation as Maya and her companions stood on the precipice of the unknown, the abyss yawning wide before them like the gaping maw of some ancient beast. The darkness seemed to press in from all sides, its weight bearing down on their shoulders like a burden too heavy to bear.

"We've been expecting you," a voice echoed through the darkness, its source shrouded in shadow.

Maya's heart pounded in her chest as she stepped forward, her companions close behind. They had come too far to turn back now, too close to the truth to let fear hold them back.

"What do you want from us?" Maya demanded, her voice ringing out into the darkness.

The figure chuckled, a sound that sent a chill down Maya's spine.

"We want nothing from you, Maya," the figure replied, its voice low and melodious. "We are merely the guardians of the truth, the keepers of secrets long forgotten."

Maya felt a surge of anger rise within her at the figure's words. They had risked everything to uncover the truth, to bring light to the darkness that had shrouded their lives for so long, and now they were being told that the truth was not theirs to claim.

But she pushed aside her anger, her fear, her doubt, and stepped forward, her eyes fixed on the figure before her. She knew that they had come too far to turn back now, that they had a duty to uncover the truth and bring it to light, no matter the cost.

"We will not be turned away," Maya said, her voice steady despite the fear coursing through her veins. "We will uncover the truth, no matter what it takes."

The figure regarded Maya for a long moment, its eyes unreadable in the darkness.

"Very well," it said at last, its voice soft yet filled with a quiet menace. "But know this: the path ahead is fraught with danger, and the truth you seek may not be what you expect."

Maya felt a shiver run down her spine at the figure's words, but she pushed aside her fear and stepped forward, her companions at her side. Together, they stepped through the veil of shadows, ready to face whatever lay beyond.

As they disappeared into the darkness, a single point of light burned bright against the night—a beacon of hope in a world consumed by shadows.

DINGS N DONGS

And so, the journey of Maya and her companions came to an end, but their quest for truth had only just begun.

About the Author

Pratham Prateek Mohanty is the Founder and CEO of Writistic Studios. Along with that, he is a fantastic storyteller and story developer. After writing four successful e-books, "Dings n Dongs" is his fifth work as an author. Through this book, he wants to imply to the readers, "Stories are meant to be made beautiful. If the characters can make you simp over them; if their story relates with yours, then you win as a reader, and I win as an author".

About the Publisher

Writistic Studios is India's youngest content production house that aims to revolutionize the art of storytelling.

A completely remote workspace spread across India, that provides one of the finest work experiences while having the passion to do it.

Writistic Studios is very much inspired by Marvel Studios, and they aim to provide scintillating storylines for a connected storytelling experience.

www.ingramcontent.com/pod-product-compliance
Lightning Source LLC
Chambersburg PA
CBHW031440130726
47989CB00003B/1227